THIS BOOK
BELONGS TO:
DATE RECEIVED:

Deep in the ocean, in the coral reef, among the shipwrecks and seaweed, the ocean creatures live and play. Here is what happened to them one warm and sunny day.

Courtney is a crab who seems to get very agitated. Every time a boat goes by it makes a loud noise and makes a complete mess of her house. Courtney ends up spending most of her time cleaning as a result. She never has any time to have fun with her friends.

Not only that, whenever she is not cleaning, she is out getting food, or gathering new rocks and mud for her already enormous home. All of this work and no play makes for one very crabby crab.

One day, as she was dragging some very heavy rocks to build up a new wall, Fiona asked Courtney a question.

"Courtney, would you like to take a break and come with us to the reef. It'll be fun!" she said.

"Fun!?" barked Courtney. "Who has time for fun? Can't you see I am extremely busy here?" Fiona was shocked by her snappy answer and swam away.

Later that day, Courtney was cleaning up after a boat had gone by and completely turned her living room upside down. Dryfuss, an elder fish, came by to talk with her just when Courtney was at her crabbiest.

Dryfuss cleared his throat. "Courtney," he began.

"What is it now?" Courtney snapped. "Can't you see I'm busy?"

"Well, yes," said Dryfuss "I can see you are busy. This is precisely why I think we should talk."

"There is nothing to talk about," said Courtney, "except maybe those messy, stinky boats."

"Well, Courtney," continued Dryfuss, "we are all concerned that maybe you work too hard. We think maybe you need a vacation."

"I don't need a vacation!" said Courtney. "I need another one of me just to keep up with all the work that needs to be done! This place is a mess! Now shoo before I sick my piranha on you!"

"Courtney, you are all together too CRABBY!" said Dryfuss as he swam away.

Courtney's friends had all but given up on her when Connor Crab had an idea. They discussed the plan three times so they couldn't forget, and then a fourth time, just to make sure. "We put the plan into effect bright and early tomorrow morning," said Connor.

"It's just got to work," said Fiona, "or else she'll be a crab…I mean crabby, forever!"

In the morning, Fiona found Courtney tidying her doorway.

"I found the perfect rock to finish your house, Courtney, want to come and see?" asked Fiona.

"Well, okay," said Courtney reluctantly.

"Great!" said Fiona. "Follow me!" Fiona waved to her friends who were hiding behind some ruins. As soon as Courtney and Fiona were out of sight, the rest of the gang got to work.

"How much further is it?" asked Courtney. "We've been gone for hours and I still don't see these rocks!"

"I thought they were right here!" said Fiona. "I guess someone else got them first. Let's go back."

The whole way back Courtney complained about how much time had been wasted when she could have been making her house better. When they arrived, Courtney saw that her friends had built her house perfectly! Inside it was clean and she had a six month supply of food in storage.

"What is all this?" asked Courtney.

"Well, we thought if we helped you, maybe you would relax a little and have some fun with us," said Connor.

"Maybe you're right," sighed Courtney. "The problem is, now that I have no work to do, I can't remember how to have fun."

"No problem!" said Connor. "I know exactly what to do!" So they danced for the rest of the day. And the next day too, and so on, until they couldn't dance anymore.